THE Queen's ORANG

First published by
HarperCollins Children's Books in 2015

10 9 8 7 6 5 4 3 2 1

ISBN: 978-0-00-813512-6

HarperCollins Children's Books is a division of HarperCollins Publishers Ltd.

Text © David Walliams 2015
Illustrations © Tony Ross 2015
Cover lettering of author's name © Quentin Blake 2010

The HarperCollins Children's Books website address is
www.harpercollins.co.uk

Printed on G Print Matt 150gsm, produced by Arctic Paper and supplied by Paperlinx
Printed in the UK by Bell & Bain Ltd, Glasgow. www.bell-bain.com

MIX
Paper from
responsible sources
FSC FSC® C007454

FSC™ is a non-profit international organisation established to promote
the responsible management of the world's forests. Products carrying the
FSC label are independently certified to assure consumers that they come
from forests that are managed to meet the social, economic and
ecological needs of present and future generations,
and other controlled sources.

Find out more about HarperCollins and the environment at
www.harpercollins.co.uk/green

-UTAN

Illustrated by the
artistic genius

Tony Ross

HarperCollins *Children's Books*

For Barron
and Snowdon.
D.W.

To Wendy, Klaus,
David, and all those
who idle at Goya.
T.R.

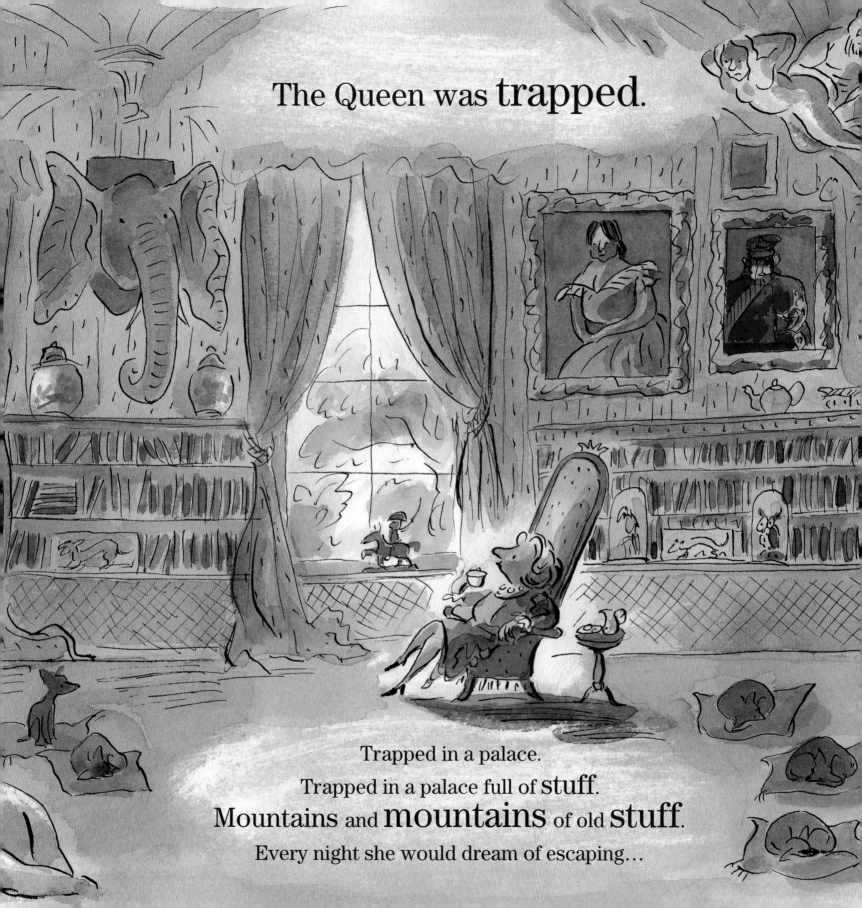

The Queen was trapped.

Trapped in a palace.

Trapped in a palace full of stuff.

Mountains and mountains of old stuff.

Every night she would dream of escaping…

The Queen had so much **stuff** that when it was her birthday no one had a clue what to give her. But this year she knew **exactly** what she wanted.

"A solid gold, diamond-encrusted stairlift?" guessed the prince.

"No!" snapped the Queen. *"Guess again!"*

"A great big bottle of brandy…?" hiccupped a red-nosed duke.

"Nooo!" said the Queen, in a telling-off tone he had heard many times before.

"...One's own orang-utan!"

A shocked silence descended
before the Duke raged,

"You want a giant MONKEY?!"

Finally, the royal baby spoke up for the whole family.

The next morning the entire royal household gathered together to celebrate.

HAPPY BIRTHDAY!

A gigantic cake the size of a paddling pool was wheeled in.

Next, the huge oak doors swung open to reveal…

The great ape lolloped in,
clambered up the silk curtains,
before leaping on to a swinging chandelier.

Finally, the orang-utan let go…

and dived into the cake with a giant plop!

The Queen **smiled** to herself.
This was turning out to be her best birthday **ever.**

Later it was time for the Prime Minister's weekly visit to Buckingham Palace.
Secretly, the Queen thought the man was an awful bore.
He prattled **on** and **on** about **himself** all day.

"I am **sure** to go down in **history**..." he prattled.

"*Tea, Prime Minister?*" interrupted the Queen.

"...as the **greatest** leader this **country** has **ever** seen, you know..."

On and **on** and **on** he prattled as the Queen's new butler wheeled in the tea trolley.

The orang-utan then proceeded to **slurp** some tea from the pot…

before **emptying** it over the Prime Minister's head.

"Milk and two sugars, isn't it?"

said the Queen.

That afternoon Her Majesty was having her portrait painted for the thousandth bum-numbing time.

"May I say how majestical your Royal Majesty looks on this most glorious of days, your royal birthday…" creeped the royal portrait painter.

He was the creepiest creep in a long history of creepiness.

But this particular afternoon Her Majesty requested some paint, brushes and a canvas be set out for her new butler too.

After a while the Queen stood up to examine the two paintings.

"Oh yes, one's orang-utan has captured one perfectly. Let's hang this one in the grand banquet hall."

"Hmmm… Yours shall be put in a dark and distant downstairs loo."

"I thank Your Highnessness for her graciousnessnessness…"

That very night the Queen had to host yet another **boring** banquet at Buckingham Palace for **all** the leaders of the world. The Queen had to sit next to the President of the United States of America.

Her Majesty found the little man an ENORMOUS pain in the bottom.
For a start, whatever delicious dishes the Queen served,
the President always demanded 'a portion of fries
on the side'. Even with his pudding!

But tonight Her Majesty knew just what to do to liven things up.
She arranged for her new butler to join in the after-dinner entertainment...

...dancing with the Royal

Ballet Company.

The next morning the maid brought the Queen her breakfast
on a silver tray as she **always** did.

"Good morning
Your Majesty,"
she chirped as she
opened the huge
velvet curtains.

Except it **wasn't** the Queen in the bed.

Oh no.

"AAAAAAAAAAAAAAAAAAAARRRRRRRRGGGGGGGGHHHHHHH!!!!!!!!!!!" screamed the maid.

It was the orang-utan!

Meanwhile, outside Buckingham Palace
a figure was swinging across the courtyard
on a jungle vine of union jacks.

It was…

But the Bearskin Guards
could not do a thing.

The Queen was free.

All the Queen left behind was a letter...

*I hereby decree
that my orang-utan butler
should be made King
and should be in charge of
everything henceforth herewith.*

Goodbye forever.

SIGNED:

Her Royal Highness

The End

A big thank you to all the lovely people who helped to make this book possible, including:

Comic Relief   Miranda Hart   Paperlinx

Rob Brydon   BORN Group   Blue Box

Bell & Bain Ltd

Comic Relief is a major charity based in the UK, with a vision of a just world, free from poverty. It works tirelessly all year round to help make this vision a reality. And in the years since it started out in 1985, with the support of some remarkable people, it has achieved amazing things and raised over £950 million.

Thank you to everyone who buys a copy of this book.
The money it raises will help people living incredibly tough lives in the UK and across Africa.

This is a photo of David and Philip taken at a Comic Relief funded project in Kenya.
Philip has played a huge part in inspiring David to continue to raise money for Comic Relief. Photo © David Hogan, 2011

**To find out how you can get involved and raise money for
Red Nose Day go to www.rednoseday.com**